WEST
JAMES ANDREW

WEST
Published by Rising Star Studios, LLC. Edina, Minnesota.

ISBN 978-1-936770-72-4

Book layout by Phillip Walton
Cover Design by James Andrew and Phillip Walton
Chapter Illustrations by James Andrew

First Edition

For Jaz

Hannah: *(skeptically)* "Is all of that really true?"

Jasmine: "Well, it helps if you have an imagination."

Chapter One

Hunching his shoulders, Christopher Wilks leaned into the driving wind. The rain stung at his face and his coat hung heavy with moisture. He swung around and began to walk the other way, finding it easier.

It didn't really matter which way he went along the highway. He didn't know where he was going, and he had no destination other than that it had to have that thread—the barest of qualifications—of being "somewhere else."

He felt a vague sense of deprivation in not having a car. The repossession of it some weeks back didn't seem to matter much to him now. There had been a string of other, more significant repossessions, the most devastating being those of his confidence and of his courage. It was as if someone had come for those in the end as well with the obligatory legal paperwork and demanded the keys.

And now it was raining harder. And it was cold.

As night came on, the concrete-gray skies darkened to black. Chris turned up the collar of his sport coat and wondered why there was no top button in the design. The jacket was fairly useless for bad weather, and he felt ridiculous wearing it.

As he sloshed through puddles, his black Thom McCann's did not protect his feet from the wet and cold. "Poor planning," he spoke the words out loud, reflexively. "Should've worn hikers."

He had learned long ago that if he made critical pronouncements himself, it was much easier than hearing someone else say them. "Yep, I'm just a poor planner, that's what I am." But Chris wasn't too hard on himself about it. He didn't have the energy. And by now he was thoroughly soaked, and his mind was teetering on the brink between caring terribly about that and not caring at all.

Chris stopped walking and for awhile

simply stood with his head bowed in the steady rain. He had a sudden thought to check the inside pocket of his sport coat and was heartened to feel a wadded lump that proved to be an old blue handkerchief. He found it was just barely large enough to tie around his neck, which he promptly did, filling in the gap there where his jacket didn't close as best he could. For the brief- est of moments, Chris tried to tell himself that the scarf made him look dashing. But he didn't ever really believe the compli- ments he gave himself.

Finally he looked up and scanned the highway in both directions for cars. He stuck out his thumb and immediately felt like an idiot. It was such a simple thing to do— just face the oncoming cars and make a fist with your thumb sticking out. But it all felt so ridiculous. So awkward. So wrong. The pose needed conviction, and he realized he didn't have any.

Giving up, Chris reached up with both hands and tried to close the collar of his jacket against his neck in a useless attempt to keep out the rain. He began to walk along the shoulder of the highway. An occa- sional car would appear and momentarily light his way. Too fast it would speed into the distance, taking its noisy illumination with it and leaving Chris to trudge along in the dark.

After a while Chris noticed a pattern and was mildly fascinated by it: light approaching from behind, getting brighter, dazzling the falling rain around him, casting a long shadow of himself ahead of him as he walked, then his "shadow self" diminishing in length to nothing, then receding taillights and fading engine noise, and finally darkness with only the sound of steady rain hitting the pavement.

After what seemed like hours of this time/experience loop Chris was beginning to feel that he hadn't made any progress. The road seemed indifferent to his efforts, and Chris began to feel a gnawing frustration. His walking slowed down and he knew that before long he'd simply stop.

Stopping. That's what Chris knew how to do. And always did. Eventually.

As a truck rumbled up from behind, Chris stopped along the shoulder of the highway and simply stood there, soaking wet and inert. As the headlights slowly washed over him, he noticed a soggy piece of cardboard lying against the guardrail in the gravel. He picked it up, and before the truck's lights moved on he read the one word that had been hastily scrawled in caps with a black felt marker. "WEST."

In the next moment Chris was standing again in the dark. Gripping the sign he looked up and noticed the rain seemed to be letting up.

Chapter Two

The piece of cardboard had been torn from a box and improvised into a sign by some other hitchhiker. Chris, never inventive or industrious himself, had learned to capitalize on the efforts of others. True to form, he immediately saw potential in the sign. He was cold and wet, and his feet hurt. It was time for him to settle into quitting.

Sign in hand, he sat down on one of the concrete posts anchoring the guardrail. As uncomfortable as it was, it was still better than standing, and a lot better than walking. He stretched his legs out and propped the sign on his lap, facing down the highway in the darkness.

He sat there a long time, long enough that his eyes seemed to adjust to the lack

of light. Or maybe, he thought, the sky
was simply slowly getting a little clearer.
He noticed stars, first hundreds, then
thousands of them, white hot pinpricks
against an ink-black sky. The more intently
he looked, the more they seemed to keep
coming "online," as if some grand celestial
control panel's bank of switches were being
flipped on in the unfathomable distances.
Chris couldn't help but feel a sense of inef-
fable beauty. He felt so small. But strangely
it was a good feeling. And it had been a long
time since Chris had felt good feelings.

Headlights came up in the distance
toward him, but the car was going the
opposite way from how he had set up
his hitchhiking station. He was hit with
the car's high beams for a moment as it
approached, and for a second Chris was
blinded by the light. Then it swooshed by
into the night.

Chris followed its taillights down the
road and noticed that they seemed to be
slowing. The car did a slow U-turn in the
road and began to come back toward him.
He sat up a bit straighter, and straightened
the sign too, and in spite of himself began
to feel a flicker of hope somewhere deep

inside of himself.

The older station wagon slowly pulled past. Chris couldn't make out anyone or anything inside of it, though there did seem to be a faint green florescence coming from the dashboard lights. The station wagon stopped about a hundred feet ahead. Chris quickly got up and began to jog to the idling car. He noticed that he was still holding the cardboard sign as he ran and thought that it was a little silly. But still, he didn't drop it.

Then the station wagon began to slowly back up, closing the distance between itself and Chris. As he caught up to the passenger-side window, it rolled down, and Chris could make out an elderly couple sitting on the bench seat. The white-haired woman was driving, her dainty, white-gloved hands resting on the steering wheel. Her husband grinned widely and said through the open window, "Need a ride, son?" And before Chris could answer, the old man said "Get in!" and gestured toward the backseat. Chris opened the rear door and got in. The dome light came on and then went off as he swung the heavy door shut behind him. He found himself in the cavernous surroundings of a fifties-era station wagon.

Chris wasn't a big car buff, but he thought the wagon might be an old Rambler. He assessed the chrome fittings and well-worn aqua vinyl upholstery. The faint smell of pipe tobacco, sweet and strangely comforting, triggered memories of his grandfather.

A quick glance over his shoulder revealed a luggage compartment full of what looked like well-worn camping equipment. The amount of tent poles, crates, and boxes seemed impossibly more than a station wagon could hold. It suggested the feeling of being in a house that looked small from the outside but whose interior was mysteriously, inexplicably large.

Chris noticed that his damp clothes were beginning to dry out in the toasty heat of the station wagon and he was glad for that. He wrung out the neckerchief over the thick rubber floor mat and retied it around his neck. Meanwhile, The Mister and Missus in the front seat seemed to content themselves with letting him acclimate to the surroundings.

He was grateful that they hadn't

immediately engaged him in conversation. He had been expecting a barrage of questions; questions he knew he had no real answers for. And then Chris surprised himself by clearing his throat and asking, "Where you goin'?"

For a moment there was no response. All he could see were the backs of two snow-white heads of hair, perched above the bench-style seat back like two fluffy birds. And then, without looking backward, the old man simply said, "West."

Chapter Three

Chris awoke in the dark to the mesmer-
izing sounds of the station wagon tires
buzzing on pavement and the dull rumble
of engine. He found himself stretched out
on the backseat, warm and dry, with the
sensation of being covered in a blanket. But
there was no blanket.

With his head down at seat level, Chris
couldn't see the old couple, but he could
hear their voices murmuring in a give-and-
take rhythm. The conversation had the
easy tone of two people who had known
each other for years and shared a deep
comfort with each other's company. Even
though Chris couldn't make out all of what
they were saying, he felt some of their
comfort spilling over him and making him
feel strangely reassured. Lying on the big

backseat in the dark evoked a vague feeling of being a child again in the complete, all-encompassing care of loving parents. He was still not quite fully awake, and the overall sensation he was having was like emerging from a pleasant dream that one tries to make linger as long as possible.

Chris continued to lie there without making any indication that he was awake. Turning his head he looked out the window above his feet and saw nothing but pitch black. He could see a faint green-glow coming from the dashboard. He had no idea what time it was, or for that matter how far they had travelled. His first instinct was ask the couple, but he quickly settled on the idea that it really didn't matter.

Chris closed his eyes and burrowed his head a little deeper into the pillow he had made with his folded arms. Drifting off to sleep, he went searching again for the pleasant dream.

When he awoke, the growing light of day filled the cabin of the station wagon. He heard the animated sounds of an argument, but clearly not a quarrel. He couldn't follow all of it, and it seemed that The

Mister and Missus lapsed into something that sounded like Latin or maybe Italian.

The Mister: "Of course notations were present. You've forgotten."

The Missus: "I haven't forgotten. My memory is like a steel trap."

The Mister: "Yeah. Rusted shut."

The Missus: (a courtesy laugh) "Guido of Aressa... Okay, I've forgotten which century."

The Mister: "Ha! It was the Eleventh!"

The Missus: "Doesn't matter. I do remember he spoke of neumes of two syllables persisting excessively without an admixture of some of three or four syllables."

The Mister: "Here we go. The Mensural-ist argument."

The Missus: "Call it what you want. Dear Guido said one neume proceeds like a dactyl, another like a spondee, and a third in iambic manner. And you see a phrase now like a tetrameter, now like a pentam-eter, and again like a hexameter."

The Mister: "He *was* a dear, wasn't he?"

The Missus: "Yes he was. And so was his wife. What was her name?"

The Mister: "I can't remember."

The Missus: *"Ha!"*

The conversation continued like this for what seemed like hours. The couple engaged in more heated discussion around words that were opaque to Chris, like *equalist-accentualist* and *polyphony* and impassioned references to people like St. Ambrose and Abbess Hildegard of Bingen. And there were the flights of an almost musical Latin/Italian. There was a lot of good-natured ribbing and laughter.

Through it all Chris noticed that even though the two people were arguing, they afforded each other a very sweet and tender courtesy. It reminded him a little of the chipmunks in the old Disney cartoons. "After you!" or "No, I insist, after *you!*" The overall effect to Chris was that it was eaves-dropping on an arcane conversation among university dons over pints in an old English pub. And yet the two didn't really seem like academic types. Just as easily they shifted into more mundane exchanges.

"Lovely shades of green in that stand of maples, no?"

"Quite."

"How's the engine temp?"

"Running a little hot, but not unusual for

the climb we just made."

They seemed oblivious, or at least indifferent, to their backseat companion. Once, they pulled over to change drivers with nary a glance to the backseat. Chris continued to rest, drifting in and out of consciousness. It was as if he were getting the first restful sleep in his life.

He had dreams, vivid and incredibly realistic and wondrous. In one he was flying, soaring over vast and exquisitely beautiful terrains. In another he was facing a range of formidable and monstrous foes. But far from being a nightmare, the dream found him completely fearless in every exchange, winning victory after victory.

And then he rested, on a level and depth he knew he had never known before. It was an otherworldly rest that seeped into his mind and soul, healing scars and filling long-empty spaces.

Occasionally he would awaken and huddle against the door and take in the passing scenery as it unfurled outside his window. None of it looked recognizable from anything he had seen in movie or television locations. He had no idea what part of the country they were passing. Chris,

having never travelled much beyond the
city he had grown up in, could only say it
was picturesque and endlessly fascinating.

The miles rolled by. Chris drifted in
and out of periods of soothing sleep in the
cocoon-comfort of the backseat of the station wagon.

Chapter Four

Chris awakened to music coming from the radio. Or rather, from the radio being scanned through a series of signals as The Missus twisted the knob. Chris had no idea where they were. A quick glance out the window indicated a rural landscape with nondescript features.

The radio snippets seemed eclectic in the extreme as she continued to fiddle with the tuner. He heard a clip from what sounded like African drums and choir. The next moment it was the shrill sound of Tuvan throat singing. That was followed by a brief snippet of what sounded like Russian folk music. The Missus stopped momentarily on a fifties-era radio comedy. That was followed by a clip from the middle of Steppenwolf's *Born to Be Wild*. At

that, The Mister said, "Crank it up!" which
The Missus was all too happy to do. Chris
pulled himself up to a seated position and
watched as the two were head bopping and
loudly singing along with the radio.

> *Get your motor runnin'*
> *Head out on the highway*
> *Looking for adventure*
> *In whatever comes our way*
>
> *Yeah, darlin'*
> *Gonna make it happen*
> *Take the world in a love embrace*
> *Fire all of your guns at once*
> *And explode into space*

Chris was a little stunned at the elderly
couple's athleticism. The Mister was
pounding the big steering wheel—and
other places on the dashboard— as if he
were a twenty-year-old drummer in an
arena rock concert. The Missus was gyrat-
ing and hollering out the lyrics into a pink
hairbrush she pulled from her purse and
was now wielding as a microphone. They
leaned their heads together and shook
their white shocks of hair and belted out

the lead in unison:

> *I like smoke and lightnin'*
> *Heavy metal thunder*
> *Racing in the wind*
> *And the feeling that I'm under*

For a moment Chris was truly worried that in all that thrashing and head banging no one was actually driving the car. And it did swerve a little. But in an instant The Missus grabbed the side of the wheel with her free hand to steady it as The Mister continued to flail around with imaginary drumsticks.

> *Like a true nature child*
> *We were born*
> *Born to be wild*
> *We can climb so high*
> *I never wanna die*
> *Born to be wild*
> *Born to be wild!*

In the big finish, the old couple began laughing uproariously and turned to look at the backseat and saw their ashen-faced passenger. This made them laugh even more until finally, catching her breath, The Missus calmly fluffed her hair back into place and said, "Good morning, Christopher! Did we wake you up, dear?"

Chris took a deep breath and scanned the highway ahead. The road was clear and fairly straight, nothing but trees and fields and what looked to be a pale blue ridge of mountains in the far distance. As he thought about it, he didn't remember introducing himself to the couple. Besides, no one called him *Christopher* other than his parents, with the possible exception of people at the DMV and bill collectors.

"How'd you know my name?"

"Good guess?" said The Mister chuckling.

The Missus looked at The Mister with mild rebuke, then turned toward Chris, her face the very picture of kindness, and said, "We know a lot of things, Christopher. It's not important *how* we know. I'm sure you have a lot of questions. What really matters is that you have the *right* questions."

Chris didn't know what to make of that, so he said nothing.

"Did you have a nice rest, son?" asked The Mister. Chris, turning to watch the passing scenery said, "Uh-huh. I did. I've never slept so well in my whole life. I must have been very tired."

"Weary, worn, and sad," The Missus sang softly, to no one in particular. Chris had a faint recognition of the lyric. It was like something from a long forgotten dream. As he was searching his mind for the rest of the song, The Mister said, "Feel like stretching your legs?"

Without waiting for an answer, he pulled the old station wagon into a turnout at the side of the road and shut off the engine. The three of them got out, and Chris immediately was taken by the natural beauty of the area.

They followed a path that wound its way through a grove of trees to the edge of a clearing and a pond with a sturdy dock at its edge. An ancient wooden boat was tied up to a bronze cleat. Across the open cockpit were two worn red oars, crisscrossed. Chris stood at the dock railing and drank in the tranquil scene.

"Our family had a boat like this once," he said without looking at them, "when I was boy. Every Memorial Day weekend we took vacations together on a lake. We rented a little cabin there, but we had our own boat that my dad brought with us on a trailer."

Chris's memories were tugging at him, imploring him to go somewhere he realized he didn't want to go. But for some reason he felt powerless to resist the pull. He was surprised that he was even sharing these things with complete strangers. But he found something entirely comforting about being in their presence. It was as if they knew everything about him anyway, so it would be pointless to withhold any part of his story.

Chris watched the subtle ripples forming around the boat as it ever so slightly pulled at its mooring. The glistening rings, like echoes of his long-forgotten past, spread out in ever-increasing arcs.

The water became a reflection pool of memories, many of them dark and troubling. Faces appeared, one after another in the expanding rings. One was his father's, full of fury and cruel rejections, growing larger and more threatening as the circle widened. Then he saw his mother's face, the familiar indifference that bordered on callousness. Faces of teachers and employers mocked him with expressions of criticisms and condemnations. In other rings, he saw the disdainful face of his wife in scenario after painful scenario. The parade of perpetrators' faces continued, one after another, until the bile was beginning to rise in his throat.

For years Chris had explained almost gladly his personal failures as an irrefutable narrative: a cruel father, an emotionally distant mother, a hyper-critical wife, unappreciative and vindictive bosses. Blaming others came intuitively to Chris. It was, ironically, one of the things he was truly good at.

Chris wanted to, *desperately* wanted to, play the victim. He knew the part well. The familiar feelings of hurt mixed with something approaching rage reflexively started to rise up within him. Finally as the faces began to fade, Chris's eyes began to well up with tears and he said, "It's... awful what they did to me."

The Missus said, "Yes, it was Christopher."

An ally, thought Chris. He tried to collect allies whenever and wherever he could.

As Chris continued to stare into the fading circles, new faces began to appear, as if at that moment a handful of pebbles had been tossed into the pond. Surprisingly, the faces were his own. He saw his *own* faces appear one after another—fury, rejection, criticism, callousness, vindictiveness. He saw his *own* portraits of cruelty and contempt toward his family. His own face striking the same poses and assuming the same contortions of hate and ugliness he had just seen before in others. It was a mirror he had never been willing to look into, and now that he had, the pain was excruciating.

He started to turn away from the watery reflections when he was caught and held by the arresting, penetrating gazes of The Mister and Missus. Though he resisted with all his might, he found himself involuntarily turning back to his portraits in the pond.

"It's awful what you did to *them*," said The Missus. Chris was stunned. He had been expecting unconditional sympathy from the kind, old couple. They had been the very picture of grandparently acceptance. And now this— the intimation that Chris was not guiltless.

And yet surprisingly, he could see no

condemnation in their eyes. In an instant it was all so clear. The indictments he had for years so meticulously logged against others' accounts, he now knew he must tally to his own as well.

"You're right," he said, "You're *right*." Chris struggled to keep back the tears. The Mister put his hand on his shoulder as they stood speechless, looking into the water. Chris began to weep softly and then couldn't help himself from falling to his knees. The Mister and Missus knelt alongside him, arms around his shoulders.

Nothing was said for a long time until finally The Mister reached into the pond and cupped a handful of water and gently poured it over Chris's bowed head. It ran down his face, mingling with his tears, falling silently into the earth.

The gesture would have seemed very odd if it hadn't felt so wonderful. The Missus was humming softly the tune Chris had been trying to remember.

And now it seemed that the lake and the very landscape itself were humming the tune. A bit of a phrase seemed to materialize in his mind. "...Lay down, thou weary one, lay down Thy head upon My breast."

Chapter Five

The three of them returned to the car in silence. As The Missus switched off with The Mister to take the wheel, she suggested that Chris might want to sit in the front for a while to get a better view. He inched in the passenger's seat while The Mister settled into the back seat, where he stretched his legs out across the aqua blue seat. He produced a pipe and fixings from an inside pocket of his cardigan and promptly lit it up. The aromatic tobacco soon filled the cabin with drifting wisps of sweet-smelling smoke.

The three of them drove for an hour without much conversation. Chris mainly looked out of the window and took in the unfolding panorama of scenery as the car rolled on through pastoral countryside.

Chris wasn't familiar with this highway
and was glad to be on what seemed to be a
quiet, rarely used back road. They passed
an occasional farm house, but he never saw
anyone in the yards—or, for that matter,
any other cars or trucks on the road either.

He did notice how beautiful the scenery
was becoming the further they got out into
the country. The contrast with the gray
city he had left behind was intense, and he
realized he had been fighting a slight sense
of disorientation. Somehow, it was as if he
had never really fully, entirely *seen* green
hills and blue skies and vibrant, living trees
before, or at least had never fully appreci-
ated this natural beauty. A growing sense of
wonder overtook him.

His senses seemed to be intensifying
to a heightened level, leaving him almost
giddy. Once, a large flock of brilliant red
birds appeared outside his passenger-side
window, for several moments pacing the
station wagon's speed. Chris was transfixed
by their exquisitely intricate markings.
He made eye contact with those closest
to his window. He felt that their glistening eyes reflected a sense of recognition
as they looked in and saw him. Then in a

flourish they wheeled away, leaving Chris breathless.

"Did you see that?"

The Missus replied softly, "Gorgeous, aren't they?"

"It was if they knew me!"

"Of course they did, dear."

Chris thought for a moment that she was humoring him, or maybe even mocking him. But the smile on her face seemed to be genuine and at the same time almost grave. The whole incident left him unnerved. Something wonderful and inexplicable was happening to him. But he was largely unfamiliar with wonderful feelings. He really wasn't sure how to process them. And so, he gave up trying to make sense of everything and settled in to simply being along for the ride.

The sky gradually turned to an encompassing purplish dusk, and Chris was a little surprised when The Mister, who was driving at this point, pulled off onto a dirt road and shortly after stopped the car. Without explanation the two elderly people got out and promptly began to unload things from the tailgate, as if they had done this hundreds of times before.

Chris could see that they were setting up
a campsite. They unfolded camp chairs
and dragged out cargo chests, each item
apparently assigned to a prearranged spot.
Soon, two marvelous tents stood where
only moments before the elderly pair had
been standing in a pile of multicolored
canvas and various metal poles. There was
something almost magical about their
machinations that left Chris simultaneously impressed and amused.

Helpless in such work, Chris thought he
would take the opportunity to go for a walk.
He found a trail that led from the clearing
where the two were setting up camp and
Chris followed it into a darkening stand
of trees. Soon he was surrounded by what
felt like a cathedral of moss-covered col-
umns reaching high into the sky, the upper
branches forming an impenetrable trac-
ery. A warm breeze rustled the branches
above him, and Chris noticed that his
clothes somehow, strangely, seemed perfectly suited for the environment in which
he found himself. His shoes seemed a
little softer and more comfortable than
he remembered. They were perfectly dry,
and the soles seemed to have a cushion he

hadn't noticed before. It was peculiar.

Even his sport coat took on the feel of something a little more rugged and out-doorsy and comfy, like something from an L. L. Bean catalog. Examining it closely, he noticed a subtle plaid patterning he had never noticed before. Golds and ochres emerged from the umber background. And if he wasn't mistaken, it even seemed to fit him better. The neckerchief seemed not to be so tight. And it felt downright silky. Evidently he had dropped a few pounds. Clearly the road trip had been good to him. He sat for a while on a moss-covered log and tried to take it all in as the night settled quietly upon him.

In spite of the wondrous things that had lately been happening to him, his mind soon fell back into the familiar groove of brooding over the disappointments and failures that stretched seemingly as far back as he could remember. His failed marriage was the latest and most bitter entry on the list of his botched attempts at accomplishing something in life. What was it she had said in that last conversation? "Chris, I've moved on. You should too."

He thought about that. After she had left,

he had thought about doing just that.

Moving on to him meant running away. It had always been his instinctive response when things seemed to fall apart. But most often he had lacked the courage to do even that. Until now. Until this trip west.

In this he felt the slightest modicum of satisfaction and Chris took the opportunity to slip into his depression, much like a man slips into a favorite coat. But try as he might, it seemed to elude him. How was it that he couldn't even seem to work up the all too familiar feelings of gloom?

He didn't know what to make of his strange travel companions, but somehow he felt that the pull to head west was purposeful. If this was "running away," it seemed to be just the thing he needed to do.

Then, something strange started happening to his face. It took him some time before he realized what it was. He was... smiling.

Chapter Six

The smell of frying bacon roused Chris from his contemplation and led him back down the winding path to the campsite. A cheery fire was heating an iron skillet set on a portable grill. The Mister and Missus were sitting by the fire and drinking coffee on folding camp chairs that were more elaborate than any Chris had seen. They looked like something that would've been used on a 19th century African safari. They were covered in damask and had tassels hanging from several places. He saw an empty chair set up next to the couple, and The Mister gestured casually for Chris to have a seat and at the same time extended him a cup of steaming coffee.

"Take a load off, son," said The Mister.

"He already has," said The Missus.

"Ah. Right you are!" said The Mister.

Chris managed to actually increase the bare beginnings of a smile he was wearing into something that seemed quite convincing. He settled himself comfortably into the ornate chair and stretched out his legs, propping his feet on one of the large rocks that ringed the fire.

"We'll have dinner a little later. We always start with coffee and bacon. Mind?" Chris had never smelled anything so delicious in his life. It was as if the coffee were fresh roasted, brewed, and extracted in the finest café in Milan. And he said just that in his enthusiasm.

The couple simply smiled and looked at each other as if to say, "Poor dear. He's never experienced anything fine, has he?"

The Mister retrieved the bacon from the skillet with a pair of silver tongs and placed it into a pan that was sitting on a small folding table. As a piece would cool and harden, he would daintily offer it to either Chris or The Missus first, and then would take a piece for himself. Chris crunched on a warm, thick piece.

"I've never had bacon this delicious. Pretty amazing!"

The Mister said something back but his mouth was full at the time. Chris thought he said something about "Serrano."

Dinner followed some time later. The only light in the camp came from the cooking fire, which cast deep shadows of the seated figures onto the station wagon and tents and gear behind them. The Mister and Missus were a choreographed *pas de deux* of culinary magic, producing pans and plates of exquisite food and drink from seemingly nowhere. The astonishing thing to Chris was that they seemed to play it off as if it were no big thing. He lost track of the number of courses as the meal stretched languidly into the night. After a dessert of something that The Mister literally whipped up in seconds, the three of them relaxed with one last serving of coffee around the dying fire.

The embers glowed in the gathering darkness, illuminating not much more than their mellow faces.

It was some time before The Missus spoke. "It's a glorious evening, isn't it Christopher?"

"Christopher? Nobody's called me that in a long time."

"But it is your name," The Mister added confidently.

"Ah well. Just Chris is good enough."

"No it's not. You know what your name means, Christopher?" The Missus asked.

"No, not really. What?"

"Christopher means 'Christ Bearer,'" explained The Mister.

"Kind of strange name for a kid, huh?" Chris quipped.

"You realize you were named after a saint, don't you?" The Missus added

Chris sipped his coffee. "I guess so. St. Christopher, huh?"

"How St. Christopher rose to such fame is a phenomenal story. His name was originally Reprobus. He was part of a Roman military unit called The Third Valerian Cohort of Marmantae," explained The Missus.

The Mister interjected, "Northern Africa, third century AD."

The Missus continued, "Reprobus was one bad hombre. His name literally means, *evil man* in Latin. He was a seven-foot tall Canaanite with a face like doom."

"He went on a search to find the toughest warlord he could find to fight for. In his wanderings he came across a band of marauders led by a villain who actually claimed to be the devil. 'Great', thought Reprobus. 'Can't get more monstrous than that! Sign me up.' But when he saw his new master panic-stricken at seeing a wayside cross and found out that *the devil* feared anything to do with Christ, he left him and enquired from other travelers where he might find Christ."

At this The Mister stirred the coals with a poker and instantly the fire flared up.

"The journey eventually led Reprobus to the desert cave of a wizened Christian hermit who instructed him in the faith," continued The Missus. "One day, near the end of his training he asked the hermit how he could serve Christ. When the hermit suggested fasting and prayer, Reprobus replied that he was hoping to be able to do something using his physical size and strength. The hermit then suggested he could serve Christ by helping travelers cross a fast moving nearby river. It had been the case that many had drowned in the attempt. Christ would be pleased if you helped prevent these deaths, the old hermit assured him."

The Mister picked up the story. "After
Reprobus had performed this service for
some time, a little boy asked him to take
him across the river. The river was running
high and during the crossing somehow
the child seemed as heavy as lead, so much
so that Reprobus could scarcely carry
him and found himself struggling to not
be swept away by the torrent. When they
finally reached the other side, he said to
the child: 'I've never been put to so much
risk. I don't think the whole world could
have been as heavy on my shoulders as you
were.' The child replied: 'You had on your
shoulders not only the whole world but
Him who made it. I am Christ your king,
whom you are serving by this work.' At that
the boy vanished."

"Reprobus, now adopting the new name
of Christ-bearer, Christopher, later vis-
ited the city of Lycia and there comforted
the Christians who were being martyred.
Brought before the local king, he refused
to sacrifice to the pagan gods. The king
tried to win him by promises of riches
and by sending two beautiful women to
tempt him. None of that worked. In fact,
Christopher convinced the women to

become Christians, just as he had already
done with hundreds in the city. Enraged,
the king ordered him to be killed. Various
attempts failed, but finally Christopher
was decapitated."

"Christ-bearer. You have a venerable
name, Christopher," said The Missus, "and
a prophetic one."

Chris said nothing, but merely stared
into the fire. He wasn't sure what all of that
meant and was somewhat fearful of asking.

Later that night, as he began to fall
asleep, he wondered if he hadn't already
been dreaming. As he drifted off, he felt
as if a soft warm blanket was tucked in
around his soul.

Chapter Seven

When Chris awoke again, he was stretched out on the big backseat of the station wagon. He didn't remember getting into the car or even breaking camp. And the recent events with the old couple seemed to diffuse and blur into hazy memory. The passage of time was similarly indeterminate. He really didn't know if he had been on the road for a few days or a few weeks. He did have a sense that they all were clearly travelling westward with little to no deviation.

Looking out the windows, Chris noticed that the scenery had undergone a change. The tree-studded hills and picture perfect farmlands had given way to an endless panorama of prairie, as if their vehicle were a boat sailing on a rippling, green ocean.

Immense cloud castles towered up into brilliant blue sky. The seafaring effect was further enhanced by the fact that the station wagon was smoothly rising and falling in a wave-like rhythm as it moved across the endlessly green landscape.

Chris lay on his back across the backseat and observed that it seemed like hours since The Mister and Missus had spoken. But he had the distinct impression that actually they were communing very deeply, without words, and together were drinking in the splendor of the passing vistas. He drifted off again to the hypnotic vibration of tires on pavement.

He awoke to the improbable sound of the clanging of ships bells and steam whistles. In a moment he realized it was coming from the grille of the station wagon's dashboard radio. This was followed by an old-timey men's quartet with organ accompaniment singing *I've Anchored My Soul in the Haven of Rest*. An emcee languidly announced, "Ahoy there, shipmates. Eight bells and all's well."

"This is First Mate Bob with the crew of the Good Ship Grace, coming to you from Los An-gull-eez, California."

The forties-era corniness of it all
touched a well-developed sense of snark,
but Chris resisted offering up the cyni-
cal comment that formed in his mind. It
was just as well. The Mister and Misses
were listening intently as the gospel quartet marched through a series of hymns.
Midway through the third, Chris had had
enough and said, "Mind if we listen to
something else?"

Without looking backward, The Missus,
who was driving at this point, exchanged
glances with The Mister. He reached for
the knob and began to scan through the
channels, stopping on otherworldly music
played by an impossibly large orchestra.
Chris noticed that there were choral parts
sung by what seemed to be thousands of
voices. Incredibly, the music sounded as if
it all were being improvised, with certain
instruments stretching out into jazz-like
leads. Chris had never heard anything
remotely like it. He rearranged himself
into a seated position and leaned on his
folded arms across the top of the front seat.
"Would you mind turning that up a little?"
he said.

To his astonishment, without a word

the old couple nonchalantly began rolling down their windows in unison. As they did, the music increased in volume until it became thunderously loud. Chris very slowly let go of the front seat and sat back, ashen-faced. The music and the inrushing wind seemed to be one and the same. It literally blew his hair back. It felt as if the sky were falling down on him. It wasn't so much the volume but the *weight*. In the impact he felt as if his soul itself were literally coming apart.

But whether it was destruction, or liberation, Chris was unable to grasp. Finally he summoned the courage to speak, or rather, shout to be heard. "Uh, would you mind turning that *down* a little?" Again, without a word or a glance backward The Mister and Missus simultaneously cranked their windows back up until the wind stopped and the music had resumed a background level.

Chris sat quietly for a long time and contemplated a kind of dread he had never known before. He felt terrified, but not afraid. In the end, he would not have minded at all if they had tuned back to Captain Bob and the Good Ship Grace. In fact, he would have preferred it.

Occasionally The Mister and Missus would pull off the road and exchange places behind the big steering wheel. Sometimes they would all take the opportunity to get out and stretch and even walk short distances if the surrounding landscape were suitable.

Once on one of these little roadside walks The Missus took the opportunity to say, "Breathe, Christopher, BR-E-E-ATHE!" At this The Mister and Missus took it on themselves to demonstrate the action for Chris, starting by bowing low to the ground, then swinging their bodies upright as they inhaled remarkably large draughts of air. Then this would be followed by fairly deflating themselves again into deep bows. After a few of these repetitions, they would look cheerily at Chris as if to say, "See? Easy!" Chris smiled broadly, but he knew intuitively that he really *hadn't* known how to breathe. And he knew that they were speaking of something beyond the physical act of filling lungs with air.

For the first time in his life Chris felt as if he was being in-filled, infused with… something that was filling a place very deep within him. He wouldn't have been able to explain it, but it was like oxygen for his soul. He knew he *did* need to learn how to breathe in the wondrous gift.

Chapter Eight

Chris had no idea how long it had finally taken to cross the sea of grass. He had lost all sense of time. Once he had glanced at his wrist, curious as to what hour it might be only to notice that his watch was gone. Stranger yet, he wasn't completely sure if he had been wearing it when he had set out on the journey. Chris had noticed that The Mister and Missus weren't wearing watches, and the clock in the heavily chromed dashboard of the station wagon was evidently broken. Chris was vaguely aware that they had experienced a cycle of days followed by nights, but even that seemed out of kilter somehow, almost as if they were artificial backdrops to the events he was experiencing.

Time. The more he thought about it, it

seemed as if things were occurring without a sense of time elapsing. The normal background track of life's ticking clock that he had become inured to was simply gone. Chris knew something was missing, but he couldn't put his finger on it. The feeling was so profound that he had almost stopped and patted all of his pockets, like a man who tries to remember where he had left a small personal object, like a cell phone or a set of keys, something that one always carried with him but now was misplaced.

Strange and wonderful things were happening, but time wasn't "passing." He remembered sunrises and sunsets. But not necessarily in that order. It made no sense and Chris knew it was hopeless to understand it, let alone be able to explain it to anyone if he ever had the chance.

Taking the back roads to the west, he had expected things to be new and different, even startlingly different. He understood that he was a stereotypical urbanite. He even expected the pace to slow down, that he might possibly be able to unwind from the manic, agitated life of the city.

But this was... different. There was *no*

time. It was as if one of his standard-issue senses like sight, or hearing, was gone. Strangest of all was that the missing sense was being *replaced*. By what, he couldn't have possibly described. How does someone explain the sense of sight to someone who has been born blind?

Something inexplicable was happening to him and it seemed fairly pointless to try too hard to figure it out. The feeling was of being in way over his head, and it gave him a sense of vertigo. It felt to him as if he were being carried along, somehow and somewhere, by an irresistibly powerful tide. The panic of that had finally started giving way to something strangely close to peace.

He thought about his lost watch. "It was a crummy watch, anyway," Chris told himself.

Chapter Nine

The prairie had begun to give way to low mesas that stair-stepped upward in elevation; the road winding in lazy switchbacks and slow climbs. The sandstone cliffs seemed to Chris as if some titanic artist had carefully hand sculpted and painted them in crimson. Chris caught glimpses of side canyons that darkened to deep reds and maroons as they deepened and twisted back on themselves and out of view.

Soon Chris noticed they were paralleling a fast-flowing river as the road wound its way up into the mountains. In places the roadway crossed and recrossed over the tumbling water yet Chris never observed a bridge. The Mister was driving now, and Chris observed a confidence if not a bravado as he commanded the car along a breathtakingly steep roadway that had no shoulder. Chris hesitated to look out the window. His fingers he realized, had been gripping the top of the seat in front of him, and his knuckles were turning white. The old station wagon seemed anything but sluggish as it powered up and up through ever-narrowing passes. The Mister and Missus seemed carefree and cheerful as ever, making Chris all the more unnerved.

Chris tried to keep his head down. He hadn't realized before that he was bothered by heights. Maybe it was because he had never been on such steep mountain roads before. He began to perspire, and he tried to untie his neckerchief so he could wipe his face but found that the knot would not come loose. He used his sleeve instead. Chris closed his eyes and tried to put the anxiety out of his mind.

To his dismay, the station wagon actually seemed to be picking up speed. It lurched and drifted wider on each curve, spitting gravel against the undercarriage as it hurtled forward. Curve after dizzying curve was coming faster now, and Chris was sliding the length of the bench seat from one side to the other. The Mister and

Missus were sliding too, the only difference being that they were enjoying it.

"Nice one!" said The Missus.

"I can get closer!" said The Mister.

"Bet you can't!" said The Missus.

"How's *that?*" said The Mister.

"Yeahhh!!" said The Missus.

When Chris would dare to open his eyes, he often would see nothing but blue sky out the side windows as the rear tire briefly hung off the edge of the road until it found traction again. Quickly closing his eyes again, Chris hung on for dear life. Then, he began to feel as if he was falling down an elevator shaft. The tire screeching stopped. His eyes popped open, and he saw nothing but blue sky out the windows. He held his breath as they fell for what seemed like an impossibly long time, long enough for the nose of the station to slowly angle downward. By now Chris was screaming, but no sound was coming out of his mouth. Incredibly, the old couple were laughing hysterically. Chris felt as if he were strapped to a gigantic WWII era bomb as the ground was rushing up toward them. He squeezed his eyes shut one last time waiting for the explosion.

It never came.

The station wagon arced forward, swooping in an elegant curve and leveled out. The roadway ahead became a runway of sorts through lesser peaks. The car lightly settled onto the pavement with a graceful thump, continuing on, to all appearances like an old station wagon driven by an elderly couple out for a Sunday drive.

The Missus glanced in the back, and seeing Chris with his head bowed asked, "Are you all right, Christopher? I hope you're not getting car sick."

"Yeah," The Mister chimed in. "Just had the carpets cleaned."

He looked back at Chris with a broad grin and seemed to be in no hurry to turn and look back at the road. This made Chris even more alarmed, but he stammered a weak "No, I'm fine. Fine. Maybe you should look where you're driving though."

The Mister smiled even wider and gave Chris a wink, still not turning back.

"Oh you're incorrigible!" said The Missus to The Mister. She reached over and took the wheel with one hand and with the other gave The Mister a solid slug on his arm. At this The Mister feigned unbearable pain and commenced to howl and moan, finally returning to his driving.

Through it all he was grinning broadly. "You're not funny at all, you know that?" said The Missus. "Can't you see the poor dear has acrophobia? Let's pull off the road and let him get some fresh air."

Right on cue a pullout appeared on the right, a wide spot that seemed to be cantilevered out over a precipice, creating a truly breathtaking viewpoint. The view was framed by an ancient railing of beautifully fitted stones forming a series of little gothic arches. The Mister pulled off the road and turned off the engine.

Turning to the backseat, he looked very gravely at Chris.

"I'm sorry son. That *was* terrible of me." Chris couldn't help but notice though that the old man seemed to be trying with all of his might to be holding back laughter.

As they got out of the station wagon, The Missus said, "C'mon, Christopher. Let's get away from that mean ol' man." At this the dam broke and The Mister roared in laughter until tears filled his eyes. He doubled up in spasms all the while waving Chris and The Missus to go on ahead. "Besides, I want to show you something," she said and took Chris's arm and crooked hers around it.

Chapter Ten

Chris and the old woman began to walk in the direction of what looked to be a wayside shelter built into the stone railing. As they got closer, Chris noticed that the gabled roof of the little hut was covered in deep moss. On one side it had been built into the mountain, and it was impossible to tell where the rocky hillside stopped and the stone building began. He noticed an old wooden door that looked as if it hadn't been opened in years, maybe centuries. Thick vines partially covered both the door and the surrounding stonework. The little building was clearly the destination where The Missus was taking Chris. He was secretly glad she had a firm grasp on his arm because he still was a little shaky from the height. He was relieved that The Missus seemed to be steering clear from getting too close to the railing. He could tell the drop off was unimaginably deep.

When they stopped at the threshold of the stone shelter, Chris noticed that the ancient door had intricately carved iron strap hinges that looked as if they had been hand forged. One hinge attached across the top and the other across the bottom, but the latch or handle appeared to have broken off a very long time ago. "How do we get in?" said Chris.

"Normally, one can open the door only from the inside," said The Missus. Chris was puzzled by her response but he didn't say anything. The Missus clearly seemed to be familiar with the place, and she left Chris for a moment and went straight up to the door. She wedged her fingers into a crack between the door and the stone jamb and gave the door a surprisingly stiff push with her shoulder. As the heavy portal opened, she said, "It wasn't completely shut, Christopher, although it hasn't been used in a very long time."

Chris followed The Missus into a vestibule that opened onto a long gallery pierced along an outside wall with a series of gracefully arched openings that were similar to the arches in the stone guard railing but much larger. Through these Chris glimpsed picture-framed views of sky and clouds. He was alarmed to find no protective railings at the edge of the floor-to-ceiling openings, and the unnerving vertigo returned to him. He intuitively moved away from the edge as far as he could as he continued to follow close to The Missus.

In time the arched windows ended, and the residual light behind them faded as the hallway led into total darkness. Chris's eyes were struggling to adjust and at first the only thing he could see was The Missus' back, glowing faintly as she disappeared into the gloom ahead. Chris hurried to stay as close to her as he could. He was tempted to grab on to her clothing as she led him along at a quick pace in the dark. How she could see in the inky blackness, he had no idea.

Their footsteps echoed loudly as they proceeded on the stone floor. Then, to Chris's relief The Missus had somehow, without breaking stride, produced a small flaming torch and held it high, illuminating the stone walls ahead. It gave off a small hissing sound and created a fine smoke that vaguely smelled of incense. Weird shadows danced around them on the walls of hand-hewn stone as the light of the flame moved on.

"Stay close, Christopher," said The Missus.

"OK, sure," said Chris, trying to sound casual in spite of his growing apprehension. "Where are we going?"

The Missus didn't look back. She said something over her shoulder that sounded something like "Toll booth."

That can't be right, he thought, but he felt it prudent not to ask again.

Eventually the hallway led to labyrinthine corridors angling off in every direction. In the light of The Missus' torch Chris noticed ancient plaques with curious inscriptions in a language he couldn't read. Each plaque seemed to label one of the corridors. The Missus kept a steady stride and gave little attention to the myriad of passages they were passing. It was evident that she knew where she was going and had a sense of resoluteness that Chris found reassuring.

Then The Missus came to an abrupt halt. Turning to face Chris, she said "You've got be brave now, my dear. Whatever you do, resist the temptation to turn back." The sense of gravity in her tone made Chris's heart pound. Before he could even utter any protestation The Missus had slipped behind him, and he felt her nudging him ahead into one of the tunnel-like corridors that appeared in front of him. With the guiding torch directly behind him, he was startled to lose sight of any feature of the passage ahead—just his shadow absorbed into the darkness. And now the torch itself was extinguished. Chris felt the small hand of The Missus give a faint pat on his shoulder as if to say, "It's all right. I'm here, and I'm not going to leave you." Under the circumstances it was the best he could hope for.

Several yards in the distance Chris heard someone speaking in the pitch blackness in low, guttural tones. It was unintelligible but unmistakably threatening. The Voice echoing in the stone corridor made Chris's blood run cold. He froze in his tracks but almost immediately heard The Missus whisper behind his ear, "You can do this,

Christopher. Just keep walking." Her hand on his shoulder never wavered as they both moved forward together into the inky darkness.

Suddenly the low mutter rose in volume as Chris evidently came into close proximity to the thing/person. Chris was dark-blind and could only surmise what it was. The growl articulated first into curses, then obscenities, and finally to grandiose profanities— all on a level of such masterful command of the language that it made Chris's mind reel. The superior intelligence of the Thing was evident, and made Chris intuitively cringe in its presence.

The Missus' grip on his shoulder tightened as she propelled him along the tunnel singlehandedly. But the Voice now was moving forward as well, inches away from his ear, close enough to feel its breath. But it had no breath. This made Chris more terrified than ever. The smell of dank decay was intense.

"I know you! Wilks, is it? Why, you miserable, pathetic little piece of feculence!"

Chris was startled, but what the creature said next stunned him. "Liar. 883,563 times you didn't tell the truth. 643,786 of those times was to protect your miserable, wormy hide."

The Voice proceeded to list dates, names, and circumstances with startling precision. All the while Chris kept moving forward under the insistent hand of The Missus pushing on his shoulder. But the voice stayed locked inches from his ear.

"Coward. Wimp. Self-absorbed. Greedy. Cruel." With each name came more astronomical numbers, dates, and places. By now the creature's voice had lowered to an uninterrupted whisper, more of a supremely confident purr than a roar. It was utterly devastating in its accuracy of accusation, almost as if some fantastically brilliant surgeon were wielding a scalpel and flaying Chris alive.

It went on. "Fool. Failure. Weakling. Worthless." Each name was legitimately interchangeable with his own.

Sometimes the Voice would shift in midsentence and perfectly mimic people Chris had known. His father. His mother. His wife. And a host of others Chris immediately recognized. The people's voices were literally being summoned up from the past and were as real as if they had been

recorded and played back on a high fidelity
digital device.

"Stupid. Hopeless. Loser. Idiot. Useless."
By now the thing's singular voice branched
out to a score of others, all speaking over
each other, but all clearly understood. It
was a gauntlet of voices reverberating off
the stone walls. "Arrogant. Prejudiced. Apa-
thetic. Lustful. Vain." The Voice described
situations and locations, all notated in law-
yerly detail. " I'm not even going to mention
what you *thought!*"

Through it all The Missus said nothing. If
she hadn't practically held Chris up as they
went forward he would've collapsed under
the weight of the assault.

It's true! It's all true! thought Chris as he
stumbled forward through the blackness.

"We haven't even really started have
we, *Wilks?* I believe I'll let you take it from
here." Chris now heard his own voice somehow, inescapably convincing and accurate,
being channeled through the creature. A
string of clips from conversations from
throughout his life poured out of the thing's
mouth like a sewer emptying into a dank
alleyway. The most hateful, vicious, pro-
fane, and cruel things Chris had ever said

echoed in the tunnel, one after another, relentlessly. They were like successive hammer blows, and in spite of The Missus' support, Chris was driven by them to the stone floor.

Now the Voice let out a dry, rattling laugh, and Chris, slumped against the wall of the tunnel, began to weep.

In the dark he heard the rustle of chains and sensed that The Missus was moving in the dark. Then he heard her say, "Enough. The boy's a Christ-bearer by name and by confession." The Voice's caustic laugh was abruptly muffled. The Missus added matter-of-factly, "We'll be leaving now."

In that instant, a blindingly bright light exploded, illuminating the entire length of the hallway. As Chris's eyes adjusted to the intense brightness, The Missus began to help him to his feet. Chris heard a noise and looked behind him. Inches away he saw a shriveled, emaciated creature with boney arms pinned and limply hanging against the wall in manacles. The thing couldn't have been more than two, maybe three feet tall. Its large head was sagging and lolling back and forth on a scrawny neck, eyes tightly shutting out the painful light.

But still the Voice boomed, unchanged in its imperious tone. "You're doomed, Wilks!"

The Missus simply helped Chris to his feet and without a glance backward calmly walked him a short distance to a door that now stood clearly in the light at the end of the tunnel. Passing through it, Chris found himself again in the open air.

The station wagon was parked nearby with the motor running. As they approached it, Chris, still visibly shaken by the encounter, quietly asked, "Who was that? *What* was that?"

The Missus replied, "It's all that's left of a once mighty personage. All he has left is his voice, really."

"What he said was true. All of it," said Chris quietly. He was still perspiring and ashen-faced from the brutal ordeal.

As they climbed into the car, some unspoken understanding clearly passed between The Mister and The Missus. The Mister turned off the engine, and The Missus turned to face Chris in the back-seat. "It wasn't *true*, Christopher. It was merely *factual*. It's what he left *out* that matters."

"What did it possibly leave out?" asked Chris.

The verbal gauntlet of accusation he had just endured had been devastating in its thoroughness. He couldn't begin to imagine anything was unstated.

"That you are Loved. Forgiven. Exonerated. Cleansed. Restored. Graced. Favored. Enthroned." Something changed in The Missus' voice as she uttered these words. Chris heard a magisterial tone, an authority, a gravity in the delivery that made him feel the words physically as much as hear them. As stunning as the Voice's accusations had been, The Missus' statements were even more so. Chris's head fell back on the top of the seat, his mind reeling.

The Mister started the engine again and eased the station wagon back onto the road.

Chapter Eleven

Mile after mile of landscape unfurled past the windows as the travelers settled comfortably into a long and uninterrupted leg of the trip. The vehicle was slowly climbing again through wooded hillsides with vast stands of tall conifers that gave occasional glimpses of glistening blue lakes.

As exhilarating as the scenery was, Chris couldn't help but meditate on the wondrous experiences he had encountered. He found himself re-living each word his mysterious companions had spoken to him and found that they were surely keys to unraveling the deep, unresolved issues of his heart.

The Missus swung the station wagon off the highway onto a smaller road with tall grass fringing the edges of the pavement. They wound their way along this country road through stands of trees clad in spring-green and the occasional meadow. Chris soaked up the serenity of it all—the tranquility of his travelling companions, the soothing scenery. He realized that it was the lack of concrete and steel that was having the greatest therapeutic effect on him. His soul was untangling, unknotting, with every passing mile.

He gave in to the drowsy pull to lie down on the bench seat and drift away, to think, to pray, to dream…

It's night. The binocular headlights of the station wagon isolate the darkness all around them from the immediate view ahead. The landscape is arid. He sees weird blocks of lunar-like ancient lava beds illuminated in sharp relief. The car slows to a stop and something or someone is compelling him to step out into the blackness. The pull is irresistible.

In the near distance he makes out a faint glow that is coming directly out of a large hole in the path ahead. As he gets closer, he sees that the circular opening spans several feet in the broken lava field. He edges as close as possible and looks down into the shaft, being careful not to fall in. Bending down onto both knees next to the edge, Chris carefully peers into the shaft. It appears to be a well of some sort, telescoping into a very deep bottom that is the source of the faint light. Leaning carefully a little bit more to get a better look into the hole, he begins to feel the rim start to crumble under his weight. He grabs furiously for something to hold onto behind him but finds nothing but smooth, sloping stone. The next instant he is plummeting feet first down into the depths.

He falls long enough to register the sickening sensation experienced when an airplane drops hundreds of feet in an electrical storm—long enough to think about a horrifying impact. But terminal velocity oddly starts to reverse. His fall is actually slowing. Chris closes his eyes tight and gives himself over to whatever unimaginably strange thing is happening to him.

He feels no impact. Not even the faintest jolt.

Chris opens his eyes to find that he is standing perfectly still on a gigantic heap of something he can't immediately describe.

The shaft opened up into a massive cavern. Chris stands on the top—the very pinnacle of something gigantic and mountainous. It is emanating the glowing light that he had seen from the lava field, which now seems impossibly high above him.

A trail of sorts, broken and winding, leads down the mountain, and Chris promptly descends it. As he walks, he is able to get a better view of the vast number of shale-like slabs that make up the mountain. In some places he sees what appear to be man-made objects wedged in among the rubble.

Chris bends down and notices a small metallic object half covered in a fine, powdery dirt. As he digs it out, he holds it up for a closer examination. Like everything else that made up the mountainous pile, it glows with a faint light, providing enough illumination to clearly see its every detail.

Chris immediately recognizes the object: a World War II-era samurai sword still in its wooden scabbard. He can make out the carefully carved initials RCW filled in with faded black ink. Chris is stunned. It was the sword his grandfather had kept in a basement storage area. On Chris's twelfth birthday his grandfather had given the sword to him with a little speech about honor and duty. Chris had promptly lost it playing "war" with other kids in his neighborhood. He had forgotten it completely. Until now.

"Grandpa's sword..." he says softly, memories flooding his mind. He thinks about how careless he had been with something that now he attributes great value to. He remembers the little speech now, too. He realizes his grandfather's challenging message has been lost as well. The excitement he feels over these discoveries is now being tempered by a growing sense of regret.

He carries the sword along with him, hilt up, being careful not to drag the curving scabbard in the dirt as he continues his descent.

At further stops he discovers more of the detritus of his youth—a rare silver commemorative coin given him by his Uncle Bill. He also remembers that he had lost the coin, but rather than confess his carelessness, he had lied that a neighbor boy had stolen it from him. Chris finds a leather bracelet he had made. Still visible was his name, which he had burned into the leather with a wood burning kit in Cub Scouts. Again, he had lost the bracelet somewhere along the way.

*As he walks along, he finds many other
things he had carelessly lost, and now years
later, he remembers them as great treasures.
These he continues to pile up in his arms as
he winds his way down the mountain.*

*After a while he notices what looks like
petroglyphs, inscriptions, and even photo-
graphic images incised into the shale-like
material in a myriad of forms. Chris stopped
to examine one closer. He could make out
the portrait of a young girl, in her early
adolescence, smiling a bit of a crooked grin,
stamped onto the surface of a small frag-
ment of shale. He instantly recognizes her
and exclaims "Charlene!" He unloads his
armful of treasures and gently picks up the
rock, smiling back at the girl's face as he
holds the portrait close.*

*He is transported in time. The memo-
ries compressed, holding their story from
beginning to end all in a singular moment.
Boy meets girl. Boy loses girl. Boy gets girl
back. Except Chris's version was always
the same—no third, redemptive act. It was
always, "boy meets... boy loses..." Scanning
around, Chris can't help but notice several
other faces scattered in the shale, faces of
different ages and with different names. All*

found. All lost. Chris sorts through these vignettes, holding each one closely to his face, as if by doing so he could somehow force the images to reveal their stories more thoroughly.

The pain is accumulating. Eventually he thinks better of looking at anymore of the portraits. But as he begins to gather up his earlier finds, his eyes freeze on one more picture. Chris closes his eyes to blot out her picture, but the mental image actually intensifies. It is Gail, dearest Gail, wife, now ex-wife. Her eyes lock onto his and speak wordless volumes of fleeting happiness and lasting regret. Tears come, first to his eyes, and then to hers.

Chris can't take it any longer. He drops the fragile piece and it shatters. He moves down the trail, wiping his eyes with his sleeve. He passes the galleries of a lifetime of loss.

He descends through a hillside of slender, shiny obsidian monuments that look like a graveyard terracing its way downward. On each monument he sees an inscription etched into the stone, some quite lengthy, others merely a single word. "DIGNITY" says one. "HOPE" says another.

Ahead he sees an area with

countless markers bearing the chiseled word "DREAMS." Each of these has a small subscript indicating a date. Under these are paragraph-length inscriptions, obituaries, outlining the various deaths of Chris's dreams and aspirations. Some have dates going back to when he was a younger, more optimistic man.

He pauses at a few of these and unearths the sad memories long forgotten. Chris wanders through these markers and feels the misery of each of the losses, like stillborn children he has never been able to see grow and become mature.

He staggers on. Raising his eyes, Chris can see that this memorial field is spread down the mountainside in every direction for miles. It reminds him of movies he has seen of European war cemeteries with their neat row after row of white crosses spreading to the horizon. There no longer seems to be any path, or maybe he has simply lost it in his confused windings through the markers.

As Chris stumbles downward, he sees that the markers have become something different. On their crystalline faces are moving pictures. Chris realizes that they portray lost opportunities to give, to serve, to love

God, to love others. One after another, endless scenarios play out showing what Chris
might have been and might have done. Scene
after scene show the life Chris could have
lived, the life, he bitterly realizes, he should
have lived.

He is devastated.

He begins to feel an overwhelming vertigo
of despair swallowing him. He drops to the
ground and curls himself into a ball and
waits for... death?

But death doesn't come. Chris instead
finds himself being lifted by someone he
can't seem to see. He feels strong arms, overpowering love, and hears a voice, a song,
that wipes away tears.

Chapter Twelve

Chris slowly awoke to the now familiar hum of tires on pavement and the radio playing softly. The Mister and Missus were silent as stones. Looking up from where he was lying, he could just see their snowy heads leaning in opposite directions against the car's side walls. They were both so motionless that Chris worried they had fallen asleep. But he could see that the car was clearly centered in their lane of the roadway and taking the slow s-curves in elegant arcs. Chris leaned over the front seat and swiveled his head to get a better look at The Missus. A quick glance confirmed she was sleeping, a slight smile wrinkling the skin around her lips. He cocked his head to the driver's side and saw to his shock that The Mister's eyes were closed as well. His mouth was open in a quiet snore.

"Hey! *HEY!!*" Chris blurted and began to vigorously shake The Mister's bony shoulders, to no avail. Panic growing, he instinctively reached over to rouse The Missus, who was just awakening from all of his yelling. She seemed composed to the point of complacency, which made Chris all the more unnerved.

"Don't pay any attention to him, Christopher. He thinks he's so funny. Don't humor him." Confused, Chris looked quickly back at The Mister who by now had turned his head sharply toward him, revealing that his right eye had been open all along. The Mister let loose with his signature guffaw, and Chris, being greatly relieved, actually joined him in the laughter, though admittedly with not near the same gusto.

Before long the station wagon slowed and then pulled off the road onto a gravel drive. A weathered but sturdy lavender Victorian house stood alone at the top of the winding drive.

"Look familiar, Christopher?" asked The Missus.

"No, not really," said Chris.

The Mister eased the car into a small grassy parking area at the back of the house, and the three of them got out. Chris was struck by the absolute silence when the station wagon stopped and The Mister turned off the engine.

The Mister hardly hesitated before he bounded athletically up the back stairs and opened the door. He turned and waved at The Missus and Chris to follow before disappearing into the house. When they caught up with him, Chris found himself in a homely kitchen with a peeling linoleum floor.

"It's in the basement," The Mister told Chris.

Before Chris could ask "*What's* in the basement?" The Mister said, "Try the back stairs." It wasn't a request as much as an order.

He hesitantly took a step down onto a cramped landing that promptly turned to reveal a darkened stairwell. Narrow, open stair treads led to a basement that was roughly finished in painted cement walls and floored with carpet remnant area rugs. Furnace ductwork crisscrossed the ceiling throughout indicating an antique "octopus" boiler.

He descended the steeply angled stairs holding to a precariously skinny handrail. With each step downward Chris's sense that he had been here before increased. After ducking under one of the large darkened galvanized duct tubes and reaching the bottom of the stairs Chris knew exactly where he was.

"After-School Bible Club," Chris thought aloud. "It was run by two old women whose names I don't think I ever even knew. I must've been something like seven or eight years old. What would that have been, Second grade?"

"Third," said The Mister, who had stopped at the bottom of the stairs and was taking in the room.

"But how could it be here, in the middle of nowhere? It was just across the street from my grade school!"

"We have... capabilities, Christopher." Chris laughed a little at that, but the comment also evoked something deeper that was closer to the feeling of dread.

As Chris scanned the room he saw that it was all there. It was as if he had been looking at an old photograph: the rickety stairs, the small wooden table with child-sized chairs salvaged from an even older school setting, the plate of graham crackers and glasses of milk all around, the mismatched Bibles. Added to all of that was the instantly recognizable aroma of *eau de old house* mixed with elderly lady perfume.

Chris looked around and smiled to himself as he remembered with great fondness the time and place in his life, possibly the *only* time and place in his life that he could remember feeling content.

He drifted over to an old upright piano that leaned against the wall. "It was the older women," he said, turning to The Mister. "They were... how should I say it? ... a little strange. But they were really kind. Other kids at school said they were weirdos. I mean, the house *was* pretty creepy."

Catching eyes with Chris, and then looking past him The Mister smiled and suppressed an embarrassed grin. Chris turned and... *there they were.* The two old women were smiling broadly, extending arms and taking him into a welcoming familial embrace.

Chris stammered a hello and felt terrible that he didn't have their names at the ready. "I'm so sorry, but I-I can't — recall…"

"Just call us the Weirdos," said the slimmer and older of the two, her eyes sparkling in good humor. The other woman was wearing "cat's eyes" reading glasses held by an ornate chain that Chris remembered being fascinated by as a young boy.

"But *how*… ?" Chris wanted to say

But before he could speak, the bespectacled woman said "I'm sure you've learned by now Christopher that asking the obvious question proves to be entirely beside the point."

He bent his head slightly in assent and smiled a wordless reply. The Mister made his way up the creaking stairs while stating he'd be waiting by the car whenever Chris wanted to leave.

"Crackers, Chris?" said the first woman, gesturing for him to take a seat. Chris folded himself into the too small chair, joined by the two women who sat in similarly tiny chairs on the other side of the little table. The slightly ridiculous scene made them all laugh. But Chris had to admit the elderly women somehow maintained elegant postures for their part.

Without hesitating, he took up the

communion of graham crackers and milk and began to eat. He was stopped by a kind but piercing glance from the thin-faced woman. Chris was instantly aware of the long-neglected and nearly forgotten protocol. He bowed his head, folded his hands and found himself saying with sincerity, "God is great, God is good. Now we thank Him for this food. Amen."

Silly, he thought. He was surprised by the involuntary thought that came next. But God IS great, beyond our wildest comprehension. He is great in love and power and in a multitude of other virtues and grandeurs. And anything we know on this earth of goodness is the merest, weakest echo of His perfect and purest goodness. To stop in the course of our rather ridiculous and petty lives and recognize those things about Him and express a simple word of gratitude is beyond appropriate. To say it's reasonable is *a severe understatement.* A little shaken, he continued with his graham cracker and milk. He looked across the table at the two women and thought, *they really don't look that old at all.* If he hadn't known better, he would say that they both were in their thirties. Something in their faces appeared so vibrant, so robust, so... *youthful.*

But strangely they still retained something of the elderly matrons he remembered from his youth.

"Don't feel bad about forgetting our names, Christopher. Actually, you never knew them. At least, not our first names. I'm Martha and this is my dearest friend, Lillie."

Chris offered his hand across the table to shake the hands of each in turn. When he did, he experienced a slightly electric jolt he as he grasped their hands.

"Lillie's husband died the same year mine did, and she moved in to the old house with me. Of course, it wasn't nearly as run down as you later came to know it. We kept each other company in our mutual grief and eventually figured out that the best way to deal with our losses was to find a way to *give*. And so, the After-School Bible Club. We held those classes year after year and watched hundreds of young boys and girls come and go up and down those very stairs to meet..." Her voice broke off, overwhelmed by emotion. "To meet God," added Lillie, smiling quietly through welling tears.

If Chris had not known the sincere conviction of these two women he would've thought it ridiculous. Old women and little kids in a dilapidated basement in the poor part of town meeting *God?*

But he knew it was true. *He* had met God there. An eight year old encountering the Omnipotent Being next to the furnace boiler. He never would've been able to explain it. Or defend it. Or even to make sense of it as an eight year old.

And years later he wasn't able to do much even beyond that. He had simply taken the beauty and power of the experience and had laid it to rest somewhere in his soul, beyond retrieval.

"John three sixteen," said Lillie. The four syllables struck a deep chord of memory and recognition. "For God so loved the world... loved *you, Christopher*... that He gave..."

Involuntarily, Chris's eyes began to glisten with tears.

"... His only Son..."

Now he slipped from the little chair and onto the cold concrete floor.

"... so that whoever puts their trust in

Him..."

And then he bowed his head, just like a little eight-year-old boy.

"...will never die but will have everlasting life."

The old/young Lillie's eyes were animated and she said "It *worked*, Christopher. It worked. You prayed the prayer... 'I love you God. I agree with you, whatever you say.'"

"I didn't fully understand what that meant. But it sounded very loving and very wise. And I chose to agree with it. That worked?" asked Chris.

"Yes, it did!"

"Wasn't there more to it?"

"Unimaginably more. But that was enough."

"Jesus died on the cross for me." He heard himself softly saying this, as if it were all one word; as if it were the answer to a well–drilled question.

"That's right, Christopher," said Martha, her eyes shining. "And He would've died for you if you had been the only boy on earth."

Under the weight of an overpowering sense of awe, Chris sat back down on the small wooden chair.

"But I was just a kid."

"You were closer to understanding the truth at that age than at any time later in your life," said Martha. "It was intuitive. You didn't need to be argued into — or out of — anything. Of *course* the big blue sky and warming sunshine was God-made, was made for you because of His love— an echo of what was left from when time began, a time when people were in love with God and He gave everything He had to them."

Lillie reached over as Martha was speaking and gently placed her hands on top of Chris's and added, "That's why you're here Christopher, why *we're* here. You're on your way Home."

Chapter Thirteen

"Is this a dream?" asked Chris.

The three travelers were standing on the rocky ledge of a canyon they had walked a short distant to from the parked station wagon. The Missus was peering into the viewfinder of a very long segmented telescope that was trained onto the valley floor. All Chris could see was a silver ribbon of river glistening miles below them.

"No, this isn't a dream, son," said The Mister.

"Am I dead?"

"For heaven's sakes, no, dear," said The Missus, continuing to look through the telescope while fingering the focal mechanism. "You're *alive*. *Fully* alive. Eternally alive. You share the life that *God* has. The life He's always wanted for you to have."

Chris knew this to be true. He knew it before he asked. Every fiber of his being seemed to pulse with extraordinary beauty and power. He stood up and edged over to the precipice. Even though the cliff had no railing, Chris noticed that he didn't feel afraid.

"Who *are* you people? *What* are you...?"

"We take people to heaven," said The Mister matter-of-factly. He had picked up a handful of gravel and was taking immense delight in flinging stone after stone into the chasm. "Prep them."

"*Prep* them?" said Chris, "For what? I thought people just sit around on clouds and strum harps. What do you do, teach them the songs?"

"You have to be careful about getting your theology from *The New Yorker* cartoons, Christopher," replied The Missus dryly.

"Or for that matter, sixteenth-century court painters," chuckled The Mister.

"Remember Pablo de Casserres?" The Mister asked The Missus. "What a *gornisht*."

Breaking off from looking through the telescope, she said, "Be charitable. He was a gifted painter."

"Exactly so. But he squandered his gift. All those chubby putti with their ridiculous wings. Where was the imagination? Where was the *verve*? Now *Blake*. Blake was an *artist!* Ah, the celestial vocabulary that man had! Swirls of light! Intensity! Abstraction! Power!" said The Mister, his voice rising.

"I agree. William may've been brilliant, but he could be quite rude to his wife."

"Ha! If being polite is the standard for being a great painter, you've just disqualified thousands," argued The Mister.

This went on between them at length and turned out to be a tour de force master's class in art history, but Chris was uninterested. He was trying to absorb the new realities that had been so casually unloaded onto him. Finally he was able to break in to the conversation with, "I don't remember dying."

"But you do remember *wanting* to die, don't you Christopher?" said The Missus.

Chris made no reply. He did remember that feeling, and the reminder immediately covered his newfound joy with dark shrouds of gloom.

Returning to her task, The Missus said, "Come here, Christopher. I'd like to show you something."

Chris obliged by walking over and carefully looking into the eyepiece. The telescope was trained on the river far below them. Chris was startled to see in the close up not just the river but a bustling activity floating along on it. It was a parade of sorts, stretching along through several twists and bends in the slow-moving river. In one glance Chris could see the beginning of the convoy as well as the end of it. The Missus expertly cranked the focal knob another half turn and the image jumped to an even closer view. Chris held his breath. He was seeing snippets of his life rolling by. As the stream moved on, he saw himself, or hundreds of versions of himself rather, aging and growing—from the beginning of the parade (his birth) to the very last (his death).

It was astonishing to see himself as a child, in places and having experiences he only vaguely recollected. But it was clearly his life, day after day, year after year rolling by. He watched himself as a high-schooler becoming colder in his faith. He watched helplessly as the college-age Chris became thoroughly debauched. He saw his young adult self falter in decision after decision affecting every part of his life. To his relief, he saw some rare bright spots. He was powerless, though, in trying to linger on those scenes as they gave way inexorably to the next.

Inner thoughts accompanied the reality-show-like video. As he saw himself as a younger man, his mind was flooded with the intense awareness that he couldn't live up to others' expectations. That he wanted to was something to his credit, he thought. He genuinely wanted to help, to give, serve, please. Selflessly, if there is such a thing.

But each year's version of himself that took the stage showed intimate details of failure after failure. Here was Chris failing at his marriage. Next was Chris who was failing at his career. Eventually the last of the parade was beginning to come into the small circle that was the telescope's field of view. These last versions of Chris were blurred by the tears that had begun to fill his eyes. The heavy shroud of despair was closing in on him, darkening his view until finally he whirled around to The Mister

and Missus and cried, "Why can't I go...
Home... *now?*"

"You're not ready, son. Not nearly. You
couldn't take the shock," The Mister said
with infinite tenderness.

The Missus added, "Christopher, you
need to face some things. You need to
heal. You need to adjust your thinking. But
you're getting closer."

Chris sighed. He took a deep breath
to compose himself. In that moment he
understood himself *better* than he ever
thought possible. To see so much of his life
in one continuous glance left him surprisingly composed, if not resolute. Much of
the confusion he had lived with now was
gone. The dots clearly were connected.

Chris asked "When will we get there...
Home?" and immediately felt like an antsy
six year old on a family road trip.

"Soon, Christopher. Just try to enjoy the
ride, ok?" said The Mister heading back
down the short trail to the station wagon.
"After all," he said smiling, "when we
started out you were more than happy to
take the scenic route."

Before long they were on the highway
west again.

Chapter Fourteen

Chris was demonstratively changing, renewing; his vitality increasing. He
could feel his energy surging. Physically,
mentally, and certainly spiritually he was
gathering strength. He was becoming...
better.

And astonishingly, so was the station
wagon. As he was getting ready to climb
back into the car, he observed something
about the paint work. It had a pearlescent
gleam he hadn't seen before. The tires, previously dust-scuffed and worn, looked to be
newly installed.

A glance around the interior as he settled
in revealed even more details previously
unobserved. Chris could've sworn the
upholstery had been vinyl, worn thin and
even cracked in a few places. Now it was

clearly leather, butter-soft and with fine stitching. Even the profile lines seemed to have changed.

The car's body seemed a little more aerodynamic and low to the ground. And when The Missus turned on the radio again Chris fairly jumped at the low end jolt of a subwoofer and surround-sound speakers masterfully concealed in the door panels and other parts of the cabin. The interior smelled better, too, of that unmistakable new car smell.

Chris leaned back into the seat and smiled. He was coming to realize that clearly there were things beyond death that he simply had not been prepared for. He had the overwhelming sense that he was getting ready for something, that he was anticipating something or some*one*. It was a delicious feeling. It was as if a drum roll had started, faintly, in the distance at first, but was slowly getting louder as he got closer.

"What's it like— heaven— *home?*"

Chris was driving now. The big turquoise bakelite steering wheel made him feel small, but very comfortable at the same time— almost as if he was piloting a large cabin cruiser out on a placid sea.

"Is it true, streets of gold? Mansions and all that stuff?"

The Mister was in the passenger seat, slightly turned to be able to carry on a conversation with The Missus who had the backseat to herself. Actually, he was greedily watching as she began to fix sandwiches, Chris could tell, simply by the delicious aromas that were enveloping the station wagon.

"It's not so much a place as a Person" said The Mister. "It *is* a place, sure. But that's not what really matters."

The sandwiches were high-stacked two-handed affairs skewered with big, fancy toothpicks that had colorful frilly tufts. As The Missus handed one to Chris, he struggled to manage it and the big wheel at the same time. He had to smile at the delightfulness of the whole construction— fancy toothpick and all. He was amazed that such a perfect thing could be summoned up from the crammed storage compartment behind the back seat with what seemed to be little effort.

"Maybe a story would help" said The Mister through a mouthful of sandwich.

"Say you had a boyhood friend— your best friend in all the world— let's call him Danny."

"God is my Judge— that's what Daniel means in Hebrew," added The Missus, trying to be helpful.

"Uh, that's beside the point" chewed/said The Mister. The Missus gave a dismissive shrug and went back to enjoying her sandwich.

"Say you and Danny grew up in the poor part of town. You were inseparable. Everyday found you playing some kind of sport together, depending on the season. Baseball. Football. Basketball. Danny was really good at basketball. As the years went by he was so good that he became a star in college, and then an MVP power forward in the NBA, with all the attendant fame and wealth."

The Mister tucked the last little corner of his sandwich into his mouth, fully satisfied.

"Danny owns a fabulous villa on a private Greek island. You've never been there, you've only heard about it from him. It's beyond description, he says. He invites you—his best buddy and pal— to spend a week with him there in the off season. All the plans are made. Private plane arranged. Then, at the last minute, Danny has to cancel. But he says you can still go and spend the week there. By yourself. You say, 'Nah, that's ok. Let's do it another time. It wouldn't be any fun without you.'"

"Capiche?" asked The Mister.

Chris, who'd been looking straight ahead at the road all this time smiled knowingly and nodded. He finished a second sandwich and said over his shoulder to The Missus, "My compliments to the chef!"

"¡De nada!" she said cheerily.

Chapter Fifteen

A "Rest Stop Ahead" sign caught Chris's attention. He was in the passenger seat— The Missus was driving while The Mister was stretched out napping in his usual position on the big bench-style back seat.

"Care to stretch your legs, dear?" asked The Missus, pulling into the exit lane. "I think you'll find it helpful." She was grandmotherly to the end. As for Chris, he never felt better, or more refreshed. The last thing he thought he needed was rest. Maybe a run, yes. And just as he was thinking that the station wagon eased into a grassy parking strip that bordered an expansive park-like setting with rolling manicured lawns and occasional firs towering into the sky. The Missus and Chris climbed out of the car leaving the old man happily snoring on the back seat.

In the near distance was an old fashioned gazebo, freshly painted white and looking something like an ornate wedding cake. A singular figure was standing at the railing looking Chris's way. The Missus gave Chris a nod and he felt compelled to break out in a jog towards the mysterious figure, not particularly knowing why.

As he got closer, the person— a man dressed in an immaculate grey suit and tie— eagerly descended the gazebo stairs to greet Chris.

"So great to meet you! I've heard so much about you!" With this the man smiled broadly and extended his arms intending to wrap Chris into a warm embrace. Chris though was shocked for a moment as he saw the bare hands and wrists at the end of the crisp white shirt sleeves. There were gashes, no, *holes* going entirely though the base of each hand. The man hesitated for a split second in consideration of Chris's horror but then hugged Chris and laughed.

The Missus said, "Dimas, Christopher. Christopher, meet Dimas."

"D-Do I know you?" Chris stammered.

"No, son." The man was ruggedly

handsome with a shock of wavy greying
hair. His dark eyes glittered with intensity.
"I wouldn't expect you've even heard of
me. It's possible. Hmm. Did you ever go to
Sunday School?"

Chris immediately scanned his memory
for the possibility the man may have been
a long forgotten teacher. As he did Dimas
put an arm around his shoulder and they
began to walk on one of the several trails
that meandered through the acres and
acres of park. The Missus meanwhile sat
on the steps of the gazebo and gave a wave
that said "You two enjoy your walk. I'll wait
here."

"My parents took me to Sunday School
when I was a kid, but we didn't go regularly.
I'm sorry, but I don't remember you." Chris
said.

"I wasn't a Sunday School teacher" said
Dimas. "I was a Sunday School *lesson*."

At this Chris was even more perplexed.
They had come to the edge of a little creek
crossed by a rustic footbridge. A weathered
bench had been built at the edge of the
stream and Dimas gestured for Chris to sit.
Dimas joined him and facing the creek said
"The story tells of two murderous thieves,

outlaws and outcasts from society. Finally captured by the imperial military they were sentenced to death and crucified".

By now Chris had pieced together who was sitting next to him and the hair rose on the back of his neck. He vaguely remembered the story and desperately wanted to recall it entirely.

"Jesus was hanging there, nailed on a cross of his own, between the two criminals." As he said this Dimas made a gesture with his right hand and Chris couldn't help but notice the healed over gaping hole through the hand/wrist, unnerving him even further.

"Torturous hours dragged by draining the life from their mangled bodies. With his dying breath one of them gasped insults at Jesus, mocking him for being unable to save them. But the other criminal strained his neck to yell at the man on the other side of Jesus and said 'Shut up! Don't you fear God? We're dying here and in a moment you'll answer for that. We're getting what we deserve. But this man has done nothing wrong.'

Then he turned to Jesus, their gaze meeting, and he said 'Jesus, remember me when you come into your kingdom.' Their nailed hands were extended towards each other, almost touching, and Jesus said 'I'm telling you the truth, today you will be with me in paradise.'"

Without looking at him Chris said, "You're the thief— I mean— the man who Jesus said would be with him in paradise."

At this Dimas slowly stood up and ran his fingers through his hair. He took a few steps towards the stream and turned towards Chris. "I am the man. And so are you, Chris. We're all that man. Thieves. Liars. Haters. Cheats. We've all failed at being the people we should have been, deserving any punishment we get. But we have a savior. A *Rememberer*. He remembered *me* that day, he remembers *all of us*, each by name, and forgives us even with his last, dying breath. I'm the living proof of that!"

Tears, joyous but pained, came to Chris's eyes. Dimas walked up to Chris. Pushing up his sleeves a bit he extended his hands with the holes for closer examination. "You have these too, Chris. Your own scars. We bear these forever as marks, medals of his forgiving love so that we too may never forget."

Chris bowed his head in silence and sat there for quite some time. Then, arm and arm the two of them made their way back to the gazebo and The Missus. There they parted, and Chris and The Missus returned to the car.

Chapter Sixteen

Incredible panoramas unscrolled by mile after mile. Chris's view, framed by the chrome-edged backseat windows, was a catalog of increasingly impossible beauty. Even a thunderstorm that boiled up on the distant horizon was a thing of awe-inspiring grandeur. Black-purple thunderheads towering miles into the sky rippled and pulsed continuously with dazzling multi-colored lightning. The ensuing rumbling roar of thunder hit the station wagon with a series of concussions that caused The Mister and Missus to whoop and shout in exhilaration. Eyes widening, Chris gripped the armrest for dear life.

And then the rainbow appeared. Not merely an arc but a gigantic *sphere* of prismatic color enveloped and permeated the car and the surrounding countryside for miles in every direction. It was as if some titanic spinning disco ball had been hung in the sky. Chris was spellbound as the kaleidoscope of colored light swept over and through the cabin of the station wagon. For several moments The Mister and Missus, Chris, and everything in the interior were illuminated with polychromatic hues.

The Mister, who was driving at this point, glanced over his shoulder at Chris and said, "Pretty cool, huh!"

There were perfect spring mornings where the stops for walks along the road way were perfumed with crystalline dew on new grass. There were perfect evenings, seemingly early autumn-ish and still warm, where the three of them would camp in groves of trees the color of rusting steel. And the conversations were perfect too, deeply affecting and soul-healing for Chris. Sometimes they would talk for hours. Sometimes no one would say a thing for just as long. In either event the experience was just as wondrous and meaningful.

Once, they had found an alpine lake to camp by, and after another sumptuous

meal by the cooking fire, they followed
along a trail rimming its edge. They followed it to a promontory that rose several
feet above the lake. There the three seated
themselves on an overhanging slab of stone
and dangled their feet over the water. The
lake deepened in hue as night came on.
White stars resolved themselves in the
increasing contrast of the darkening sky.
They stayed there basking in the loveliness,
time strangely standing still.

Chris was following the arc of a comet
slowly etching itself onto the blackboard
sky when he said, "I can't seem to remember how I died." And then it was as if simply
because he *said* that he was trying to
remember, he did.

His mind started to flood with moving
images as he gazed into the dark, but they
were shadowy and indistinct. All he could
see were dark things moving against a
black background. He sensed The Mister
and Missus moving in closer on both sides
of him comfortably. The Missus slipped
something compact and metallic—a flashlight—into his hand. "Use this, my dear
Christopher."

He pointed it into the distance ahead of

him and fingered the rocker switch on. A
beam of light appeared and funneled out
to a round illumination hundreds of feet
in front of them. In its glow he saw the
dark images begin to illuminate. First he
saw an empty double-car garage, gloomy
with shadows, with its pale wood trusses
exposed over a grimy concrete floor. As
he got closer something that looked like a
duffel bag appeared, limp and lifeless hanging from a cross beam. As he played the
flashlight's beam over the scene, it seemed
to zoom in like a video camera. Suddenly
his face flushed, and then his entire body
instantly tensed with the sickening rush of
adrenaline.

The shapeless bag-like thing hanging
from the rafters was a man's body. A scarf
was knotted tightly around the neck and
stretched a short distance to the beam.
Chris flicked the beam again, and the light
zoomed in on the shadowed face. It was
canted at an unnatural angle.

The face was *his*.

He slumped down onto the rock slab,
breathing heavily. He grasped his neckerchief and fumbled with the loose knot but
only made it tighter. "It... was... *me*. **I... took**

my own life."

He was seized with the panic that accompanies terrible revelation. Suddenly every moment, every thought, every feeling that had brought him to the wooden beam was now being revisited on him. The darkness in his soul was suffocating. Yet even this gave way to a greater terror. There was no sympathy, no self-pitying to hide behind. He saw, he knew, in a blindingly bright moment of self-awareness that the taking of his own life had been an act of God-defiance. In doing so he had told God "No! I refuse the gift, and the responsibility of the life you have given me. This unique, miraculous, ingenious, spectacular creation of yours, I choose now to destroy. I refuse to trust you to help me understand it, to make it meaningful, to even get through it. I reject. I defy. I abandon. I... *I*."

The flashlight fell from his hands, the mechanism's delicate glass shattering in a hundred pieces. The vision of horror was instantly gone.

Chris lay on the stone in the arms of his friends. A sorrow and regret beyond description permeated every part of his being. He tried to speak but couldn't. He wanted to say, "I'm sorry," but he couldn't make his voice to work.

The Mister tightened his hug around Chris's shoulder and said quietly "We know you are sorry, Christopher. *He* knows you are. He knew you *would* be. And He forgave you for even this, so very long ago."

The Missus worked the knot loose of Chris's neckerchief and gently removed it. The pale skin was ringed in red; a scar that The Missus very soothingly stroked. In the starlight, the three of them wept.

Chapter Seventeen

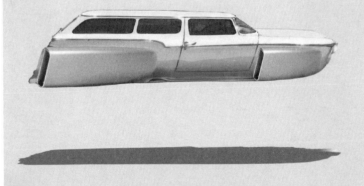

They travelled on. The westering road took them through wondrous vistas and sceneries that were, no longer to Chris's surprise, truly breathtaking. The concept of "impossibility" had effectively faded away. At a turnout where they stopped to change drivers, Chris noticed that the station wagon no longer even had wheels. Somehow they had been replaced by some kind of antigravity repellers. Chris merely shook his head and chuckled.

The mysterious "drum roll" was getting louder. It was all around and even *in* Chris. He sensed they were getting close to the end of their journey. But it was more than that. Much more. He was getting close to Home. Every part of his being thrilled.

The station wagon came up over a ridge,

and the expansive view of the ocean came into view just as the sun was beginning to set. There was no more road. It simply terminated on a sandy, grass-fringed dune just above a trail that led down to the beach. The Mister turned off the engine, and the three of them silently climbed out of the car. No one was able to take their eyes off of the setting sun. The cobalt sea lightened to a pale blue then slowly began to turn to molten gold as they stood side by side, collectively holding their breaths.

A warming breeze tousled Chris's hair. It seemed to him to be flowing from far out at sea, from the sun itself. Without looking down, he felt The Mister and Missus take his hands on either side. His heart was fairly breaking from the beauty of it all and the overwhelming sense of love that shined upon and enveloped him.

He began to cry.

And laugh.

And something in between that he certainly had never experienced before. The Mister and Missus squeezed his hands a bit harder, increasing even more the overpowering love he felt as the three gazed out across the sea.

But the sun didn't set.

It stopped.

It hung on the horizon and slowly became larger and larger, a living burning incandescence, a supernova that rapidly filled the horizon and began to overtake the sky. The warm breeze had merely been a precursor to a growing radiant wave that Chris could see was coming toward them at incredible speed. It blew the burnished surface of the ocean in an ever-increasing fan of dazzling golden spray. The roar of it was deafening. As the advancing pressure wave hurtled toward them, Chris abandoned himself to whatever was about to occur. He knew it wouldn't be death, at least not the death he had experienced before. He intuitively knew he was about to experience something more related to *life*. And rather than being terrified, he was exhilarated.

The Mister and Missus gripped Chris's hands even more firmly and stepped a little in front of him, lowering their heads and shoulders in bracing for the wind/wave, not so much to protect him, but simply to anchor him against the force.

Then it hit.

He was expecting the impact to rip him off of his feet and blast him to who knows where. But he stood firm, as did The Mister and Missus. Instead of bowling him over, the wave was somehow blowing *through* him. He was yelling at the top of his lungs in the roar, eyes clamped tight. He felt something happening to the hands of his companions. It felt like they were... crumbling. Or burning into cinder, or *what*, he couldn't possibly describe.

Against his better judgment, he forced his eyes open to see what was happening to them. In the blinding light he could make out their outlines. They were changing. The wind/wave/flame was consuming them, or at least the *outsides* of them. It was as if the sweet elderly couple he had known were being sandblasted away, revealing their true personages underneath, beings of indescribable majesty. They became bigger, stronger and surprisingly younger; or more accurately, ageless. They were still holding Chris's hands, but not with hands of flesh, but of... what? *Fire?*

Chris had no ability to tell. He dared to look down to see their hands, and in doing so saw his own hands. They were gone.

Better, they were... *replaced.*

Scanning upward, he saw that all of him was changed. The old (and dying) Christopher Wilks was gone, and a new Christopher was standing in his place, glowing, radiant, *living*. He reached to feel the rough scar on his neck and found that it had changed, too. The skin there was silky smooth. It had been transformed to a silvery band that gleamed with reflected light.

And then they began to run. The three of them with hands joined dashed into the golden surf, then on to the water, gathering speed. They ran/flew toward the Light, skimming the crests and swells of the molten-colored sea, exulting with laughter. The Missus (newly, gloriously revealed) broke away with a burst of speed. Looking back over her shoulder, she waved Chris onward. Chris saw in her eyes the exhilaration, the promise of being so close to Home after a long journey. The Mister was singing uproariously in an unknown language. But then the words became crystal clear to Chris:

"I heard the voice of Jesus say,
'I am this dark world's Light;
Look unto Me, thy morn shall rise,
and all thy day be bright.'

I looked to Jesus, and I found
in Him my Star, my Sun;
And in that light of life I'll walk,
till traveling days are done."

"C'mon, Christopher. It's your song now. Sing!"

And he sang as the three of them ran toward the sky-filling Sun.